COLLECTOR'S EDITION

This book belongs to

_____

SeaWorld and Franklin & Friends:
Exploring Nature Together

Franklin's Partner

Seaworld
KIDS

COLLECTOR'S EDITION

KIDS CAN PRESS

FRANKLIN had lots of good friends.
They all liked to play the same games.
Their favorite was Bumpy Buggies.

One day, they came up with a great idea.
They would hold a special Bumpy Buggy
race — and everyone in town could join in
the fun!

Franklin and his friends made a poster to promote the big event. Bear hung it up outside Mr. Mole's store.

"A Bumpy Buggy race? That sounds like fun," said Mr. Mole.

"It's going to be *lots* of fun," said Franklin. "But you have to make a buggy."

"And you need to have a partner, too," said Bear. "Every team needs someone at the top to push and someone at the bottom to catch."

Franklin and Bear really wanted to win the race. They decided to fix up their old buggy.

"Maybe a new paint job," said Franklin.

"Let's put a siren on top — like an ambulance," added Bear.

"A siren? Aw, Bear. Don't be silly," said Franklin.

Franklin and Bear finally decided that the buggy needed new parts. They knew just where to get them — from Fox's dad.

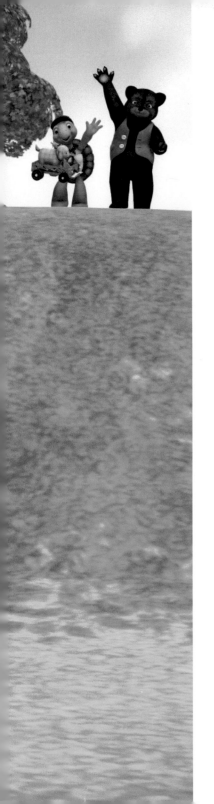

Franklin and Bear went to Fox's house. He and his father were making music with an old chime and a garbage pail.

"Hey, guys!" said Fox. "What are you doing here?"

"We need some new parts for our Bumpy Buggy," said Bear.

"Could we look through your collection of stuff, Mr. Fox?" asked Franklin.

"Sure," said Mr. Fox.

"Come on, Bear," said Franklin. "Let's look for something to make our buggy super cool-io."

"Thanks, Mr. Fox!" said Bear.

Franklin found some blue jar lids. He thought they'd make great new wheels.

"Hey, Bear!" shouted Franklin. "How about these?"

Bear ignored Franklin. He climbed into a bathtub filled with junk. Inside, he found an old airplane.

"Look!" yelled Bear. "Wings! We could make the buggy fly."

"Bear, buggies don't fly," said Franklin.

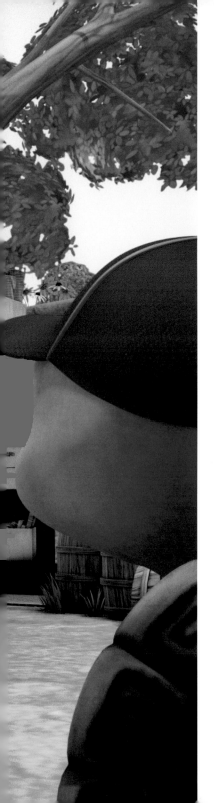

"We'll try it with wings," said Bear.
"If it doesn't look good, we'll do your
wheel thing."

Bear attached the green wings to the
buggy. "Let's call our buggy the Mean Green
Speedmobile," he said.

"The Mean Green Speedmobile?" asked
Franklin.

"Yeah," said Bear. "Look, I have to go.
You hang on to the Speedmobile."

Franklin grabbed the buggy and frowned.
He did not like the changes Bear had made.

Back home, Franklin decided to fix the buggy — the way *he* wanted. As he was putting the finishing touches on it, Bear came to visit.

"What happened?" said Bear. "You took off the wings!"

"It's a rocket now," said Franklin. "And since Sam will ride in it, I've named it Sam's Rocket."

"You even changed the name?" asked Bear.

"It's better this way," said Franklin.

"But, Franklin, we're partners!" said Bear. "That means we decide stuff together."

"*We* didn't decide on wings or 'Mean Green Speedmobile' together," said Franklin. "*You* decided all that stuff."

"If that's what you think, then maybe we shouldn't be partners," shouted Bear.

"Maybe we shouldn't," said Franklin.

Bear stomped out of the shed. He slammed the door shut.

Franklin was upset. He took Sam's Rocket and went for a walk to calm down. At the top of Thrill Hill, Franklin tripped and dropped the buggy. It sped downhill — straight for a big rock!

Suddenly, Bear appeared. He dove onto the path and grabbed the buggy.

Franklin was relieved when he saw the buggy was safe. He got up and ran down to Bear.

"I'm sorry, Bear," said Franklin. "I should have listened to you."

"That's okay, Franklin," said Bear. "I should have listened to you, too."

The two friends shook hands.

"Let's start over," said Franklin. "But this time we'll decide things together. Deal?"

"Deal, partner," said Bear.

The next day, Franklin and Bear arrived at Thrill Hill with their spiffed-up Bumpy Buggy. The two friends had decided to call it Sam's Speedmobile.

All the racers got ready. One partner stood at the starting line. The other partner waited at the finish line.

"Ready! Steady! Go!" yelled Officer Rabbit.

The contestants pushed their buggies, then cheered as they watched them fly down Thrill Hill. It was a close finish, but Goose and Beaver won the race.

"Wasn't that great?" yelled Bear, as he ran down to Franklin.

"Great?" asked Franklin. "We lost!"

"Lost? Who cares?" said Bear. "Did you see how cool-io our buggy looked?"

"You're right, Bear," said Franklin with a laugh. "I never saw a more cool-io buggy in my life!"

This Collector's Edition is available for distribution exclusively through SeaWorld Parks & Entertainment. All rights reserved.

SeaWorld Kids and Design™ is a trademark of SeaWorld Parks & Entertainment, Inc.

From an episode of the animated TV series *Franklin and Friends*, produced by Nelvana Limited/Infinite Frameworks Pte. Ltd.
Based on the Franklin books by Paulette Bourgeois and Brenda Clark.

TV tie-in adaptation written by Harry Endrulat.
Based on the TV episode *Franklin's Partner*, written by Jeff Sweeny.

Franklin

Franklin is a trademark of Kids Can Press Ltd.
The character Franklin was created by Paulette Bourgeois and Brenda Clark.
Text © 2012 Context*x* Inc.
Illustrations © 2012 Brenda Clark Illustrator Inc.

ISBN 978-1-894786-51-5
CM 13 0 9 8 7 6 5 4 3 2 1

Kids Can Press acknowledges the financial support of the Ontario Arts Council, the Canada Council for the Arts and the Government of Canada, through the CBF, for our publishing activity.

Published in Canada by
Kids Can Press Ltd.
25 Dockside Drive
Toronto, ON   M5A 0B5

Published in the U.S. by
Kids Can Press Ltd.
2250 Military Road
Tonawanda, NY   14150

www.kidscanpress.com

Edited by Samantha Swenson
Designed by Muse Communications

This book is smyth sewn casebound.
Manufactured in Buji, Shenzhen, China, in 10/2012 by WKT Company

CM PA 12 0 9 8 7 6 5 4 3 2 1

Library and Archives Canada Cataloguing in Publication

Endrulat, Harry
    Franklin's partner / Harry Endrulat.

(Franklin and friends)
Based on the character by Paulette Bourgeois and Brenda Clark.
ISBN 978-1-55453-835-5

1. Franklin (Fictitious character : Bourgeois) – Juvenile fiction. I. Bourgeois, Paulette II. Clark, Brenda III. Title. IV. Series: Franklin and friends

PS8609.N37F74 2012   jC813'.6   C2012-903139-9

Kids Can Press is a *corus*™ Entertainment company